THIS WALKER BOOK BELONGS TO:

_____

_____

_____

_____

for Mama Bear
(and our nine new big houses!)

First published 1991
by Walker Books Ltd, 87 Vauxhall Walk
London SE11 5HJ

This edition published 1994

2 4 6 8 10 9 7 5 3 1

Printed in Hong Kong

British Library Cataloguing in Publication Data
A catalogue record for this book is
available from the British Library.

ISBN 0-7445-3609-X

New BIG House

by Debi Gliori

WALKER BOOKS
LONDON

Mum says our house is so small she's
afraid to sneeze in case the roof blows off.

Dad says with one budgie, two
hamsters, the nursery school rabbits at
weekends and the lonely goldfish,
when our cat has her litter of
kittens the floor will give way.

The trouble is, now the twins can
sort of walk, the house is shrinking.

The hall is full of baby walkers and
wellies, the kitchen is full of high chairs
and laundry, and the living room
is a Lego minefield.

There's a gate on the stairs and a lock
on the fridge, and fetching a drink of
milk in the middle of the night is
becoming very difficult.

The twins wake us all up at three
in the morning and have a short party.
Dad folds himself into
their bunk ...

and they camp in Mum's bed and
sleep like starfish till morning.

One day we were all so tired and grumpy,

we decided to look for a bigger house.

We took a measuring tape, a torch, some
maps, a supply of orange juice and
a packet of biscuits.

It was like an expedition into the unknown.

The first house we looked at was huge.
Mum and Dad walked round the empty
rooms measuring, banging on walls and
shining the torch into cupboards.

The twins found a ghost in the coal
cellar and I saw lots of enormous mice
with long tails in the bathroom.

The next house had a funny smell,
and while we were eating biscuits and
drinking orange juice ...

Mum fell through the floor.

The third house had mouldy wallpaper
and big mushrooms growing in
the sitting room.

By the time the twins had found the
compost heap and we'd cleaned them up,
everyone had had enough and we went home.

At three o'clock the next morning, I went
downstairs to get a drink. Mum and Dad were
still up. They were trying to draw a picture
of our house with a bit added on. It wasn't a very
good drawing, so I helped them.

When we went upstairs, the twins wanted
to play musical beds again, but eventually
we all managed to fall asleep.

Ever since then, we've spent weekends
having big long parties with loads of wood
and nails and squelchy concrete. Mum
says it's like living in a builder's yard. Dad
says he's moving into the garden shed.

I think our new big house is wonderful.
The twins do too.
Now they can play musical rooms
instead of musical beds.

And Granny says we've got so much room,
she's thinking of selling her house
and moving in with us.

MORE WALKER PAPERBACKS
For You to Enjoy

Also by Debi Gliori

MY LITTLE BROTHER

Sometimes the little girl in this delightful story wishes her
bothersome little brother would just disappear – until,
one night, he does!

0-7445-3612-X   £3.99

NEW BIG SISTER

One moment Mum's off her food and the next she's eating
marmalade and cold spaghetti sandwiches! What's going on? Mum's
having a baby, of course. But the biggest surprise is yet to come!
Ideal for preparing children for a new arrival.

0-7445-3610-3   £3.99

WHEN I'M BIG

by Debi Gliori

A small child ponders the advantages of being big.

"Interprets every child's fears and ambitions… Debi Gliori's
illustrations are full of humorous detail which will find a wide audience
among three and four year olds." *Valerie Bierman, The Scotsman*

0-7445-3125-X   £3.99